Pup and Hound

For my mom and all our pups and hounds — S.H.

For Errol — L.H.

Kids Can Read ™   Kids Can Read is a trademark of Kids Can Press Ltd.

Text © 2004 Susan Hood
Illustrations © 2004 Linda Hendry

Kids Can Press acknowledges the financial support of the Government of Ontario, through the Ontario Media Development Corporation's Ontario Book Initiative; the Ontario Arts Council; the Canada Council for the Arts; and the Government of Canada, through the BPIDP, for our publishing activity.

Published in Canada by
Kids Can Press Ltd.
29 Birch Avenue
Toronto, ON M4V 1E2

Published in the U.S. by
Kids Can Press Ltd.
2250 Military Road
Tonawanda, NY 14150

www.kidscanpress.com

The artwork in this book was rendered in pencil crayons on a siena colored pastel paper.
The text is set in Bookman.

Edited by Tara Walker
Designed by Julia Naimska
Printed and bound in China by WKT Company Limited

The hardcover edition of this book is smyth sewn casebound.
The paperback edition of this book is limp sewn with a drawn-on cover.

CM 04   0 9 8 7 6 5 4 3 2 1
CM PA 04   0 9 8 7 6 5 4 3 2

National Library of Canada Cataloguing in Publication Data

Hood, Susan

    Pup and hound / Susan Hood ; illustrated by Linda Hendry.
(Kids Can read)

ISBN 1-55337-572-6 (bound). ISBN 1-55337-673-0 (pbk.)

1. Dogs — Juvenile fiction. I. Hendry, Linda II. Title. III. Series: Kids Can read (Toronto, Ont.)

PZ7.H758Pu 2004   j813'.54   C2003-906689-4

Kids Can Press is a **Corus** ™ Entertainment company

Pup and Hound

Written by Susan Hood

Illustrated by Linda Hendry

Kids Can Press

What was that?

What was that sound?

Hound looked around.

He sniffed the ground

until he found ...

... what made that sound!

It was small and round,

curled on the ground.

It was Pup.

He was fed up!

"Bow wow wow!"

said Pup to Hound.

"I want to eat —

now, now, now!"

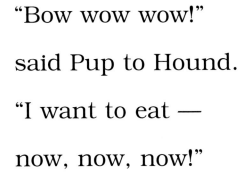

Hound looked around

until he found ...

a stick!

Ick!

A shoe?

Ewww!

A bone?

Groan!

Then Hound found

a treat to eat.

Meat!

Neat!

Pup gobbled up

all the meat.

He left nothing

for poor Hound to eat!

Never mind.

Hound chewed the stick.

Then Hound gave Pup

a good-night lick.